KNIFE EDGE

KNIFE EDGE

Robert SWINDELLS

Barrington Stoke

For all who go unarmed

First published in 2008 in Great Britain by
Barrington Stoke Ltd
18 Walker Street, Edinburgh, EH3 7LP

www.barringtonstoke.co.uk

This edition first published 2017

ISBN: 978-1-78112-686-8

Printed in China by Leo

Contents

Chapter 1

Self-defence

Hey. Sam's my name and I'm 14. I go to Orwell School in Gretley. It's not bad, but there's a gang called the Sharks. There are ten guys in the Sharks, all well hard. Cecil True is their leader. Kids laugh if you've got a name like Cecil, but no one laughs at Cecil True. If they did, they'd never laugh again. At anything.

We went to the same primary school when we were little, Cecil and me. *I* didn't know Cecil was going to be a gang leader, did I? I laughed at his name. Every day. "Want to wrestle, Cecil?" I'd say. I called him "Cess the Mess" as well. Hard to believe now.

But Cecil hasn't forgotten. He doesn't say anything, but I know he remembers by the way he looks at me. He hasn't got time to get me for it just now. He's too busy. He's got his gang stuff to do. But one day, when he has a spare minute, Cecil's going to get even. And I don't fancy that at all.

The Sharks carry knives. They don't go round stabbing people all the time. I'm not saying that. But everyone knows they carry knives, so everyone's scared of them.

I always walk home with my best mate, Tim. We both live in Prince Street. We don't hang about. We walk quickly, watching out for the Sharks. There's a little park on our way home. It's called Sparrow Park and it'd be nice to hang out in there, but we can't. We don't dare. Cecil says Sparrow Park is Shark territory. If the gang catches some kid in there, they beat him up and take his phone. If he's got one, they pinch his watch and nick his cash as well. The Sharks aren't in Sparrow Park all the time, but it's not worth the risk.

One day, Tim and I are passing Sparrow Park and Tim says, "I've got a knife."

"Huh?" I stare at him.

"A knife," he says. "Look."

He lifts up his sweatshirt. There's a great big knife stuck down the front of his trousers. He pulls it out so I can see the blade. It's long and wide and curvy. One edge has a row of pointy little teeth, a bit like a saw.

"Wow!" I gasp. "Where'd you get it?"

"Sports shop." He grins. "It's a fisherman's knife."

"I thought you had to be 18 to buy a knife," I say.

He nods. "You do. My cousin got it for me. He's 19."

"Let's have a proper look," I say.

He hands me the knife. It's heavy and the blade glints in the sun. "Gonna start fishing then?" I say.

Tim grins again. "Sort of," he says. "Fishing for Sharks."

My mouth drops open. "You're not gonna go after Cecil and them?" I say.

He shakes his head. "Not go *after*. But I'll get it out if they hassle me." He smiles. "Self-defence."

I think about it later, at home. Self-defence. No one can blame you for defending yourself, can they? And if you've ever laughed at a guy like Cecil True, you'll *have* to defend yourself sooner or later. I think I need to get a knife of my own.

I shut myself in my room, go on the internet. I google the word *knives*. There are like, a *billion* sites! I look at the first ten. They sell every sort of knife. Even swords from Japan – Samurai swords. One snag – *none* of them will sell to me. You've got to be 18 to buy from them. I swear and turn my laptop off.

I don't have a cousin. Well I *do*, but she's only seven. No use sending *her* to the sports shop to buy a knife for me. Have to think of some other way to get one.

I could pinch one of Mum's. A kitchen knife. She's got six, all different sizes. Trouble is, they hang in a row by the cooker. She'd notice in two seconds if one went missing.

I don't know what to do. As it happens, it'll be sorted soon by pure luck, but I don't know that yet. I lie awake half the night, trying to work something out.

Chapter 2

Other People's Rubbish

Orwell School has this course called Citizenship. It's about how to be a good citizen. You know. Don't hunk off school. Don't spray graffiti. Be polite. Don't drop litter. Help people.

Some of us go out two afternoons a week to do stuff for senior citizens – in other words, old people. We do decorating, gardening, fitting security chains on doors. Stuff like that. That first Tuesday, a big bunch of us go out, helping different grave-dodgers.

Our teacher, Mr Pringle – or Crispy as we call him – is in charge of the Citizenship project. He puts me with this really old guy called Jack

Conyers. First time I knock on his door, old Jack gawps at me like I'm a ghost or something.

"I'm Sam Brown," I say. "From Orwell School? I've come to help do some jobs for you."

"Oh, aye," he says, when at last the message gets to his brain. "They *told* me someone'd be coming. Any good at digging, are you?"

I shrug. "Anyone can dig," I say. "Not rocket science is it, Mr Conyers?" I'm thinking, 'Is he going to let me in, or keep me standing on the step all afternoon?'

After a bit Jack Conyers decides I'm not going to mug him. "You'd better come in," he says. "Sit down for a minute. D'you want a cup of tea?"

He's all right, old Conyers. We sit drinking tea. It's better than double Maths anyway. He says he can still do most things in the garden, but not the heavy digging. That's going to be my job.

At last we finish the tea and go outside. Conyers points to a sad old shed. "You'll find all the tools in there," he tells me. "Just take anything you need."

The garden's like a flipping jungle. Tall weeds and high, clumpy grass. I keep thinking I'll see a tiger, or a herd of elephants. He shows me the part he wants me to dig. It's the same size as France.

"Start with the fork," Conyers says. "Easier than the spade."

Then he goes in the house and I go to the shed. It's so full of stuff, I can hardly move. The fork and spade are near the front wall. There's a rake as well, and an old broom. At the back there's a saggy old sideboard. There's loads of stuff all over it – big bags of seed, plant pots, balls of string – you name it. Under the sideboard are three drawers. I pull one open.

'Interesting,' I think. 'Snooping in other people's rubbish.'

It's a really heavy drawer, with rusty tins full of nails, screws and bits of old metal. I scrabble about and shove stuff aside. It's dim in the shed, but right at the bottom something gleams, and that's how I find my knife.

I lift it out and lie it on my hand. I stare at it. It's beautiful. I don't mean fancy. It doesn't glitter like Tim's fisherman's knife. In fact, it's black all over – the blade and everything. There are no pointy teeth and it's not heavy. It's a slim dagger – a stiletto is its proper name. Both the edges are sharp – very sharp. I could carry it in my waistband and nothing would show. But I'll have to be careful not to hurt myself with it.

I've already decided to nick it. Well, why not? It was right at the bottom of the drawer. Old Conyers hasn't touched it in years. Forgotten he's got it, I expect. It's a waste, leaving it lost under all that rusty old stuff. And anyway, what would an old man like him do with a dagger? I slip it into an inside pocket of my jacket.

It's a warm April day and it's hard work, digging. I'm sweating. I take off my jacket, hang it on the fence.

'It'd cost Conyers a packet,' I tell myself, 'to get this dug over by a gardener. All I'm getting is a rotten old knife.' And that makes me feel better about nicking it.

Old Conyers brings me a mug of tea. He looks at the turned soil, all the ground I've dug. Says, "Great job, Sam, keep up the good work," and goes back inside.

I dig till home time.

Chapter 3
Schoolboy Citizens

That Wednesday morning we have a meeting with Mr Pringle. He wants to know how we all got on being good citizens.

"All right, Sam," he says when it's my turn, "tell us what you did."

But I *can't*, can I? Think about it. What would I say?

"*It was warm work, sir, digging a plot the size of France, but I did manage to nick a really good knife. A stiletto. It's here, tucked down my trousers. I intend to hurt Cecil True with it one of these days.*"

Yeah, right. What I *actually* say is, "It was all right, sir. Bit warm. I did some digging. Mr Conyers said I did a great job. Can't wait for Thursday to carry on."

"Splendid, Sam," Crispy says, and he rubs his hands together. It's all right for him. *We* do the work, and every old-age pensioner in Gretley thinks *he's* a saint. Saint Crispy.

At morning break I catch Tim by the sports block. "Got your knife, have you, Tim?" I ask.

"Course." He grins, pats the bump round his middle.

"Me too," I tell him. I whip up my sweatshirt, pull out the knife. I'm close to the wall so other kids won't see.

Tim asks to hold it.

"Hmmm," he says, as he feels it in his hand. "Light, isn't it? And sharp. Where'd you get it?"

"Took it off this kid who tried to mug me," I lie. "Last night in Sparrow Park."

"Yeah, right," Tim says. He hands it back. "You don't have to tell me if you don't want, you idiot."

"No." I shake my head. "Actually it was in the old guy's shed where I was working yesterday. He didn't want it any more."

Tim looks at me. "*Tell* you that, did he?"

"Not in so many words," I say, "but if you want something, you don't bury it under loads of rubbish, do you?"

Tea time, we walk home with our weapons well hidden.

"Two years in jail," Tim says with a grunt, "if a copper stops us."

"No copper will," I tell him. "Look at us. We're good schoolboy citizens, you and me."

After tea I go up to my room, shut the door. No one ever comes in my room without banging on the door and asking first. I take my uniform off, pull on some jeans and a top. I tuck the knife down my jeans and face the mirror.

I practise quick draws. I spin round in a crouch, stabbing and slashing. I try out mean, nasty looks as well. I scowl. I show my teeth, narrow my eyes, stick out my tongue. Make faces like I was one of the All Blacks doing the *haka* before kick-off. I growl and look in the mirror to see. I don't know what it'll do to Cecil True, but it scares *me* right enough.

Then I start thinking about this girl. Suzi Pool. She's in my year and she's drop-dead gorgeous. Sometimes I can hardly pay attention in class for looking at her. I want to go out with her, but she only likes older guys.

But one day I invited her to Pulse for a coffee. It's cool at Pulse, everyone goes there, but Suzi's like, "Get lost, Wimp – I don't date babies." *Babies.* It took me weeks to get up the nerve to ask her. I was gutted when she said that.

But I feel so good after my practice session with the knife that I decide to phone Suzi. Maybe she'll be out with some cool guy from Year 11, but you never know your luck.

She picks up.

I say, "Hi, Suzi – it's Sam."

"Sam who?" she says.

"Sam," I say. "You know, at school?"

"Oh." She sounds so bored I nearly hang up. "What do *you* want?"

"Where are you?" I say.

She sighs. "At home, *why*?"

"Fancy a burger?" I ask.

"With *you*?"

"Sure, with me. You don't have to *marry* me or anything. We eat burgers, talk a bit, I walk you home. What d'you say?"

She doesn't say anything. It goes so quiet I think she's hung up. "Hello?" I say.

"OK," she says. "See you outside Pulse in 20 minutes."

I'm so gob-smacked, I sit gawping at the phone instead of getting ready for my date with Suzi.

Chapter 4
Ten Feet Tall

At seven I'm outside Pulse in my hoodie, jeans, Nike trainers and with a hidden knife. No sign of Suzi.

'It's cool,' I tell myself. 'I'm early, and girls are always late.'

I walk up and down, but not near the window. There are kids from school inside. If Suzi stands me up, I don't want them to know.

She shows up ten minutes late. She's wearing a fringed jacket over a crop top, a skirt so short it's almost a belt, and ankle boots. She doesn't say why she's late, so I don't ask. I can hardly believe she's come at all. We go in.

Everyone looks, like I knew they would. 'Hey,' they're thinking, 'look who's with Suzi Pool.' I feel like I'm ten feet tall.

We take a corner table. I pass Suzi the menu.

"What'll you have?" I ask.

She scans the card and takes her time. "The Health-in-a-Bun," she says at last. "With an apple juice."

"Health-in-a-Bun?" I say, trying not to laugh. "That's like, salad and bread. You could get that at home."

She sighs and looks at me as if I'm stupid. "Do you think I look good, Sam?" she asks.

"Course," I tell her. "Who wouldn't?"

"Well," she says. "I don't look good by scoffing super-size cheese-burgers and triple fries. Or by drinking Cokes." She hands me the menu. "You have what you like."

I decide on a double burger with cheese and fries, mega banana milkshake. I'm not sure anyone cares if *I* look good. I go and order. Suzi checks her make-up. I watch her as she pulls faces at herself in a little mirror. Like me in my room with the *haka* earlier, I think.

I come back with the food. I sit down and stare across at her. She's picking bits of lettuce off the edge of her bun. She nibbles them and looks round. It's as if I'm not there.

"Hey, Suzi," I say. "Thanks – you know – for coming." Naff, I know, but I have to start somewhere.

She looks up. "I only came cos my mum wanted me to tidy up my room," she says. "So don't start getting ideas."

A real put-down, right? I do the only thing I can do. I shrug. "No worries," I tell her. "I was bored out of my head as well, once I finished knife practice."

"What?" She frowns.

I look at her. "Knife practice."

"What's that?"

I sigh. "Practice. With a knife. No use carrying a sharp if you're not sharp yourself." It comes out so cool, I wish I was someone else so I could admire me.

Suzi's looking at me now. "You're saying you carry a *knife*?" she asks.

I nod. "Sure. Have for years. Got to, haven't you? Self-defence."

"I …" She looks at me. "I didn't think you'd carry *anything*, except maybe a spare nappy."

My turn to frown. "Shows how wrong you can be."

"Have you got it on you now?" she asks.

"Course," I tell her. "Want to see?"

She nods. I take a quick look around, slip a hand in my jacket, take out my knife. "Don't let every man and his dog see it." I slide it across the table to her.

She hides it with her bag, sits looking at it. "Where did you get it?"

I grin. "There was a bit of a fight. Years back. Outside the football ground. Some bloke dropped it, running. I picked it up. Had it ever since." I'm amazed how all this bull comes pouring out of my mouth – I'm not even trying. And Suzi's lapping it up.

She's like, "Have you stabbed anyone?"

I shake my head. "Not *stabbed*. You'll kill someone if you stab them. But I have cut one or two guys up." What a lie. Biggest thing I've ever cut is a slice of bread.

Suzi slides the knife back to me and I drop it in my pocket. We eat. I see lads sneaking looks at Suzi and I know that they wish they were me.

It's perfect, till Heston Weston sticks his nose in. He's a Year 10. Not a Shark, but he's a big aggressive guy with a red, meaty face. I clocked him when Suzi and I came in. Him and his two mates. I've been keeping an eye on them. I hope they don't want trouble. Some hope. Heston gets up and comes over. He leans across in front of me, puts his fists on the table and blocks me out. I can't even see Suzi now.

"Baby-sitting eh, sweetheart?" Heston says to Suzi.

She giggles. "Something like that, Heston."

Heston. His mum and dad must be barmy. I mean, if your name's Weston you don't call your kid Heston, right? Heston Weston – he's got a name like a cartoon character.

Except Heston Weston's not funny right now. I don't like trouble. Any other time, I'd maybe sit still and wait till Heston got bored dissing me and left. But this isn't any other time. I've just told Suzi what a hard guy I am, with a knife and everything. I can't just sit and take it, with my knife in my pocket. I'm scared, but there's no getting away from it – now's the time to try out one or two of those faces I practised in my mirror. I take a deep breath.

"Hey, Weston?" I say.

"Huh?" Heston turns round so he can see me. "Did you say something, Titch?" he grunts at me.

I nod and slip my right hand inside my jacket. "Yeah. You're blocking my view. Back off." I hope he doesn't see how tense I am.

Heston stays where he is, laughs. "You want me to back off, Titch, you're gonna have to make me." He turns back to Suzi. "Think the little guy'll make me, sweetheart?"

Suzi giggles again. "Don't think so, Heston. He's all hat and no cattle, as the cowboys say."

"Is *that* what you think?" I jump up. My chair goes over. And there I am – crouched over the table, the knife held out in front of me. I can't really believe it.

"Hey, now hold on," Heston cries. He backs away with his hands up, gawping at my blade. "I was having a laugh, that's all, there's no need ..."

I stare at him, then down at the knife, then at Suzi. It's unreal. Everyone in the place is looking at me. Heston Weston's almost messing himself. And now the manager's coming, with back-up. Suzi's looking up at me with her big round eyes like I'm some kind of action hero. And none of it's real. Not me at all. It's like the rubbish I talked earlier has come to life. And I'm trapped in it. Sam Brown – knife man.

Mum'll *kill* me.

Chapter 5

Not the Real Me

"Take it easy, son." The manager stops just out of knife range. His two mates stop as well. "Put that thing away and leave. Do it now and I won't call the police."

I crouch behind the knife and look round. Everyone's staring at me. I hate it. All I want is for it to be over. But a part of me feels powerful. In control. All these people waiting to see what I'll do. *Me*, Sam Brown. No one's ever cared less what I did. They care now, and a part of me likes the feeling.

'Don't chuck it away,' goes a little voice inside my head. 'Not just yet.'

I point the knife at the manager and make a jabbing movement. He steps back. His back-up steps back too. I smile the tight smile I practised in the mirror.

"OK," I murmur. "We're leaving." I look around again, slowly. "No one moves till me and Suzi are out of here. Got it?"

Everyone nods. The manager looks at me. "It's cool, son," he says. "No one wants to mess with you. You won't be followed. Just put the knife away and go. I won't call the police."

I stare at him. "You're not as dumb as you look," I hear myself say. Only it's not me – not the real me. The real me feels like he's about to be sick. I give Suzi a quick look. "Come on."

How I make it out of the door I'll never know. I'm screaming inside – totally stressed out. Outside I hurry away, looking for a dark corner to fall apart in. Suzi trots beside me. Maybe I fooled her like everyone else. I hope so. But I don't want her with me in one minute's time when I totally lose it.

"Heston and his mates'll come looking for me, Suzi," I gasp. "You better go."

She doesn't argue. Doesn't stop to give me a kiss on the cheek. Just makes a *huh!* sound, tosses her head and flounces off. I'm left all on my own. No one ever does that to a proper action hero.

I find an alley that's lined with wheelie-bins. I lean on the wall near the bins. I'm shaking so much I just about cut myself as I put the knife away. Don't suppose *that* happens to action heroes either. I lean there and take some deep breaths. Trying to stop the shakes.

All the time I'm listening for foot steps. You bet I am. Heston Weston's foot steps. I made him back off. He was scared and his mates saw that he was scared of Sam Brown – the wimp. His street cred's shot to bits. He'll want to get it back together. Only way to do that is to sort Sam Brown. Sort him once and for all now. If Heston finds me here, it won't be much of a picnic on the beach.

But Heston doesn't come. I stay there ages, leaning on the wall. I take deep breathes till the shakes die down. In my head a film of what happened at Pulse is playing. I'm the star of the film. See how I crouch behind my blade. Notice how cool I look. You don't know how my guts are churning. You don't know I'm trying to hide the shakes, that I'm thinking about my mum. The film keeps on playing. Each time it plays I'm cooler, harder, more of a hero. Sam Brown, knife man. Boyfriend of the drop-dead gorgeous Suzi Pool.

I could nearly believe it myself.

"Nice time, love?" Mum says when I walk in the house.

What does she want me to say? "*Thanks, Mum, it was ace. I lost my rag down at Pulse, held everyone at knife-point. You and Dad would've been dead proud.*" Yeah, right.

What I *actually* do is mumble, "It was OK, I'm off to bed, goodnight."

In my room I have a brilliant idea. I'll call Suzi. Check she got home all right. Tell her I did too. It's been special, see? A special evening in my life. I don't want it to stop.

"Suzi?" I say.

"Oh, it's *you*," Suzi says. "I've just been talking about you."

"Yeah," I say. "Who to?"

"Cecil," Suzi says.

"Y ... you're kidding me, right? That's a wind-up, isn't it?"

"No," she says. "Soon as I got in I called him, told him everything that went on at Pulse. I wound *him* up – told him he needs to watch out."

"You *didn't*?"

"I did. He says he's not bothered but he is. I can tell. He says he remembers you from primary school. You called him names. He's been meaning to talk to you about it. I expect he will now. Goodnight, Sam. Sleep tight."

She laughs and cuts me off.

Sleep tight? I'll be lucky if I sleep at all and she knows it.

But I *do* sleep and I have this dream. I'm in Sparrow Park at night. Alone. I never would be of course, but you know how dreams are. I'm not even nervous. I'm Sam the Wham. I'm not kidding – in my dream, that's my nickname. Sam the Wham. I go to the swings. The kids' playground. Cecil True is on a swing. Heston Weston is pushing him. Heston sees me coming and starts to scream. Cecil yells at him, "*Push*, Heston, then jump on. He can't touch us."

I'm running towards the swings. My knife's in my hand. I want to cut them both. Heston gives the swing a mighty shove, then jumps on. It's going so fast, it goes right up over the bar, with Cecil sitting and Heston standing, gripping the chains. And it doesn't go over just once. It does it again and again, getting faster and faster. All I can see is a blur, like the propeller on a plane spinning round. I hear them laughing, but I can't do anything. I'm forced to stand there like a total wuss. I look round. Suzi's at the top of the slide and she's watching me. She's pointing and laughing at me. "We don't date babies," she jeers.

That wakes me up.

Chapter 6

A Few More Miles of France

After that dream, I lie awake thinking. These are my thoughts.

Loads of guys were at Pulse.

They all saw me pull the knife.

What if one of them grasses on me? The manager said he wouldn't, but someone else might do it. Heston might do it for revenge. I could be stopped in the morning on my way to school. Searched. If the police catch me carrying a knife, they'll arrest me. I'll have to go to court. Mum and Dad will love that. Not.

So. Smart thing to do, leave the knife at home. Just for a day or two. If a copper stops me, I'm not carrying. I haven't got a knife. Never had one. Plus, if Suzi really *has* told Cecil, and he wants me to fight, I can't. Not got my weapon, see. It'll have to be some other time, OK?

I get out of bed and tape the knife under my desk. No one's going to find it there. I feel a bit better. Even manage a bit of sleep before morning comes.

On Thursday morning I walk to school without my knife. I feel a bit let down that no one stops me. Cecil's not waiting for me by the gates either. Maybe Suzi was kidding me on after all.

I tense up when the bell goes. What if some guy who was at Pulse has told on me to Mr Lewis? He's the Head Teacher. I can picture him walking in the classroom with a police officer. "*Come with me, Brown – the officer would like a word.*"

That doesn't happen either. At break time, I corner Suzi in the playground. I'm like, "*Did* you tell Cecil about me?" I can't stand the suspense any longer.

Suzi's with her two mates, Karen and Lauren. She looks at them and says, "Did you hear something squeak?"

Lauren nods. "I think it was a shrimp, Suzi. There's one by your left foot."

Suzi pretends to notice me for the first time. "So there *is*." She peers at me. "Did you say something, shrimp?"

I play along. "I asked if you really did talk to Cecil last night."

"That's for me to know and you to find out," she says. Not a very good line – I think Suzi gets most of her lines off the soaps. "Come on, girls," she says and they leave me standing there like a wuss, same as in my dream.

After lunch it's Citizenship.

I go back to work in Jack Conyers' garden again. He brings me a cuppa, looks at me funny.

"You weren't in Pulse last night by any chance?" he says.

I'm so gob-smacked I *nearly* forget to lie. Nearly. I shake my head. "No. I don't go in the week, Mr Conyers. Homework, you know."

He nods. "Ah. Only my lad's the manager, see? Says they had a spot of bother last night."

I look at him. "Your lad?"

"Aye," he says. "My son, Kevin. He told me some kid pulled a knife."

"A knife?" I say. "Wow!"

"Yes," he says. "It was a commando knife."

"A *commando* knife?" I'm listening properly now. "You mean, like in World War Two, Mr Conyers?"

He nods. "Aye, lad, just like in World War Two. A real Fairbairn Sykes commando knife." He looks right at me. "Not many of them around these days, I reckon."

I shake my head again. He knows something – I'm really tense. "No, I don't suppose there are, Mr Conyers."

"Funny thing is," he says. "I had mine till just the other day. But it seems to have vanished now."

"*Yours?*" My mouth drops open. "You mean … you were a *commando*, Mr Conyers?"

He gives me a thin smile. "Oh, I wasn't *always* a silly old fart who can't dig his own bit of garden, Sam. I used to be Jacko Conyers – *Sergeant* Jacko Conyers, Commando."

All I can do is gawp at him. It's too weird – a coffin-dodger who was a hero. Why didn't he die back then when he was still a hero?

And I really wish I hadn't nicked his knife.

But there's nothing I can do about it right now, is there? Maybe I'll slip the knife back into his drawer of sad old rubbish next Tuesday.

He's watching me. "My son told me what the boy at Pulse looked like," he says. "Sounded a bit like you. That's why I asked."

"Right." I shake my head. "Like I said Mr C, I don't go out in the week. Too much homework."

He doesn't push it any further. I fetch the fork from the shed and dig up a few more miles of France.

Chapter 7

Surrounded

On Friday I leave my knife at home again. Well, no point carrying it when I'm giving it back next Tuesday, is there?

It's been good, though. Word's got around. Nobody bothered me yesterday. Nobody bothers me today either. Heston Weston's got a grudge. Cecil True always had. But they avoid me, stay away. I'm Sam the Wham. No one *calls* me that – it was in my dream – but they stay away.

I should leave it. Act cool, like nothing's changed. But I don't. It feels so good, I have to brag. Big mistake. Lunch time, I share a table with Tim and six other guys.

"Notice how Cecil keeps his head down now I'm here?" I say.

Tim's like, "Ssssh!"

The others don't say anything.

"Same goes for Heston Weston," I go on. "I faced him down, made him back off. You'd think he'd want to get even, but he keeps away." I do the tight smile. "He's not as dumb as he looks."

Like I said, I should have acted cool. There's a grass at my table, but I don't know it. Not yet. Nothing happens at lunch time or at break. They wait till after school.

It's twenty to four and Tim and I are walking home. Tim's nervous. He hasn't got his fancy fisherman's knife. He left it at home in case I get stopped when we're together. He's going on at me to be careful.

"Don't push your luck, Sam," he says. "I don't know why Heston hasn't flattened you. Or what's stopping Cecil from shutting your mouth too. But I'd keep it shut anyway, if I were you. You might have fooled some guys, but you and

I know you're not hard. You stir Cecil and his mates up, they'll have you for breakfast."

He's wrong, as it happens. They won't have me for breakfast. They'll have me for tea.

We're passing Sparrow Park. There's a low wall. Thick bushes. We hear a crashing, rustling noise and then ten guys come through the bushes and over the wall. It's the Sharks. In seconds we're surrounded. There are other, normal people about, but they keep well away.

"Now then, Brown." Cecil's tight smile is much more scary than mine. "You know me, don't you? *Cess the Mess? Want to wrestle, Cecil?*" He puts his hand on my chest and gives me a shove. "Well – the answer's *yes*, Brown. I *do* want to wrestle. In fact I've waited years." He turns to Tim. "Get lost, kid – this has nothing to do with you."

Give Tim his due. He tries. "Sam's my mate," he says. "You don't run out on your mate."

Cecil looks at him. "*You* run out, or your blood does," he snarls. "Your choice."

Tim gives me an awful look, then walks on. Can't blame him.

Cecil turns back to me. "OK, Brown. Over the wall. *Now*."

I sit on the wall, swing my legs over. I don't even think about trying to run. Two Sharks grab me and throw me into the bushes. My face gets cut and scratched on twigs. I'm so scared I hardly notice.

The same two guys grip my arms again and shove me along. There's a shelter in the park that kids use in wet weather. Heston Weston's in there, grinning. So's Suzi. The two guys let go of my arms and the gang makes a circle with me in the middle.

"OK, Brown," Cecil says. "Let's see this famous knife."

I shake my head. "Haven't got it, Cecil. It's at home."

"Haven't got it – *sir*," he goes. "Respect me, Brown – *say* it."

"Haven't got it, sir," I murmur, not daring to do anything else.

"Louder!" he yells. "We didn't hear you."

"Haven't got it, SIR!" I shout. I'm already nearly crying if you must know.

"That's a shame," Cecil says. "I don't want to think about how our knife fight'll go, Brown. When one of us doesn't have a knife."

"I don't want to fight you," I croak.

Suzi laughs.

"Huh?" Cecil frowns, looks round the circle. "Hear that, everyone? Hard man doesn't want to fight." He gives me a shove. I reel into Heston, who pushes me back into the middle.

"Well," Cecil says. "If you don't want to fight, we'll have to think up something you can do instead." He pretends to think. They're all staring at me, grinning and jeering. If I had the knife now, I swear I'd use it and die rather than this.

Cecil drives a fist into his palm. "*I* know!" he cries, as if he's just thought of something. "You can lick our *boots*, Brown. Or trainers, or shoes or whatever. Then we'll christen you *Boot Licker Brown*."

"Boot Licker Brown!" Suzi cries. "You're a proper comedian, Cess!"

I have no choice. Just thinking about it now makes me want to cry. They all stand with one foot forward. Twelve shoes. I shuffle round the concrete circle on my knees.

Twelve shoes. Twenty-four eyes looking down on me. The contempt in Suzi's eyes burns the hottest.

It seems to go on for ever. I boil with anger inside, but I won't let it show. Are they going to let me go when I've finished? I don't know. I'm surrounded.

They do let me go. Or rather, they go. They walk away. No one says anything. No one looks back. It's the most horrible, lonely, *ashamed* feeling I've ever had.

I stand up. My knees hurt and there's a vile taste in my mouth.

I trail home, replays going round in my head. The replays show me as *they* saw me. As Suzi saw me. Not a shrimp. Not *even* a shrimp. A grub – crawling at her feet, scared out of my mind.

When I get home I don't know where to put myself. How can I show up at school on Monday? Or ever again. What a terrible, terrible thing it is they've done to me.

OK – I was a fool. Why didn't I keep my mouth shut? It was stupid, I admit it. But did I deserve to lick their boots?

My head's so messed up I can't think straight. But one thing is crystal clear. It's this –

Cecil True will die.

Chapter 8

Till the Day You Die

The weekend seems to go on for ever. I stay in the house. But I can't stand to be with Mum and Dad

In one of the replays in my head, Mum and Dad are watching me crawl round that circle of feet too. At least *that* didn't happen, I tell myself. But it doesn't help much.

One thing will help. Cecil True, dead at *my* feet. Sounds sick I know, but I feel like nothing less than that will wash away my shame.

So, I make a plan. This is my plan.

Monday, I'll go to school. It'll be hell. Word will have got round. My name will be known. My *new* name. Boot Licker Brown. Guys will call me that. Girls too. Especially Suzi. And I'll take it. I'll say nothing, make everyone think I'm down. Finished. The end of Sam.

Tuesday, I'll go to work for old Conyers as normal. I'll have his knife with me, but I won't give it back. What I'll do is this – I'll offer to sort the shed. It's like a tip in there. I've finished digging France, so he's bound to let me tackle the shed next.

And here's the clever bit. While I'm in the shed, the old guy can't see me. If I slip away for a few minutes, he won't know. Cecil True's painting doors and window frames down the road on Tuesdays. I can cross a few back gardens and be with him in no time. He won't be expecting me. I'll creep up on him, knife him and go back the same way. I'll leave the knife. No fingerprints of course – I'm not daft. And if the police suspect me, Conyers will tell them, "*Sam was here when the lad was stabbed, doing out my shed. Sure? Of course I'm sure. My knife? It's vanished. I expect the killer pinched it. No, I never lock the shed."*

War hero, old Conyers. The police will believe him. And what's *really* sweet is, the kids'll know who killed Cecil. They'll know it was me. It won't be Boot Licker Brown any more. It'll be Sam the Wham. Too hard to mess with, too smart to take the rap.

Good, eh?

Monday goes just like I knew it would. Wall-to-wall slagging. I don't mind. No one'll slag me off again after Tuesday.

Tim doesn't slag me. He's heard what they made me do and he feels bad. "I should've stuck with you," he says.

I shake my head. "They'd have got *both* shoes cleaned instead of one, that's all," I say. Tim knows I'm right.

The day passes slowly, but it passes. Tim and I walk home together, same as always. Except we walk on the other side, going past Sparrow Park. No one's there.

On Tuesday morning I peel the tape off Jacko's knife, lift it from under my desk and slip it in my pocket. My plan's a good one and I know everything'll be all right. Still, now the day's here I feel a bit sick. My hands shake. A little voice in my head keeps asking me questions.

What if Conyers doesn't want the shed sorted?

What if he brings you a cup of tea and you're not there?

What if Cecil has someone with him?

What if Cecil turns round just as you go to stab him and you miss?

And what about DNA?

I say "bye" to Mum like I'm never going to see her again. As I walk along Prince Street there's a lump in my throat. I talk to myself. I'm like, *You don't have to do this, Sam. Forget it, take the slagging. Slagging doesn't last for ever.*

It's like I'm two guys. One guy's hoping Citizenship will be cancelled this afternoon.

The other can't wait for it to start. I don't hear anything the teachers say. All I think about is crossing the back gardens. Creeping up behind Cecil. Sticking the knife into him.

It's never going to happen. Two things mess it up. One weird, one stupid. Here's the weird one.

I do get to clear out the shed. I'm humping stuff out of it and stacking it on the path. Old Mr Conyers watches for a bit, then goes in the house and comes out with tea. We stand drinking, looking at the stuff on the path. Most of it wants chucking away. Suddenly he's like, "What's up, lad?"

"Huh?" I say. "*Nothing's* up. What d'you mean?"

He narrows his eyes. "You're tense, Sam. Jumpy. Something's up. Something you have to do."

I shake my head. "No." I try a grin. "Except get this lot sorted."

"Not that." He looks at me. "You're acting like my men did in the War before something big. Before an op. When they were scared but trying not to show it. What's your op, Sam?"

I want to yell, "*GET IN THE HOUSE!* There's an op all right. Operation Stab Cecil, and I need to get on with it."

"Why don't you go in?" I ask instead. "I'll just get on and clear up this shed."

He shakes his head. "*Something's* up," he insists. "I'm never wrong."

"Well," I say. "You're wrong this time, Mr Conyers. I better crack on."

And then the stupid thing happens. I take off my jacket, chuck it at the shed door. It misses, drops on the path and the knife falls out.

"Ah," Mr Conyers says. "I *knew* I was right. Come on."

He puts an arm round me. Steers me towards the house.

I'm like, "What you *doing*?"

"We're going to sit down," he says. "And I'm going to tell you a story."

It's crazy. We leave the knife lying there. I let him take me inside. A part of me wants to shake him off. Another part's glad. *My plan's messed up*, goes one part. *Thank God for that*, goes the other.

We sit across from each other, in armchairs.

"It's 1941," Mr Conyers says. "France is thick with Nazi troops. My men and I cross the Channel at night. We're going to blow up a dry dock that the German Navy needs. We'll destroy other stuff while we're at it. We're out-numbered a hundred to one. Some of us will die. We know that, and we go anyway. It's what commandos do."

He looks at me. "The dagger you borrowed is part of my gear that night. It's for quick, silent killing – and I've been trained to use it, though I hope I'll never have to. But that night I do. I have to. There's a guard hut with a telephone inside and one German soldier. He's got the phone in his hand. He might be calling up for back-up. I creep up behind him. There's a terrific racket going on outside. Gunfire. Explosions. He doesn't hear me. I throw an arm round his neck. Slip the knife in under his ribs. It finds his heart. He sighs and dies.

"I see that he's just a young lad. I lower his body to the floor, and then I spot what's on the table. He was writing a letter home. He's not finished it. There's a photo too. An oldish couple, smiling at the camera. His mother and father I expect. They look a lot like my own parents. They'll never get his letter now. Never see their precious boy again. Someone else's boy has taken him away from them."

Old Conyers looks at me with tears in his eyes.

"I was a commando, Sam," he says. "A tough guy. But I couldn't get that photo out of my mind. *Still* can't, a lifetime later. That poor lad's mum and dad, smiling. It might easily have been *my* mum and dad."

He breaks off and stares at the floor.

After a bit he says, "Everyone's someone's child, Sam. Even the people we hate. There's someone who'll grieve if they don't come home. If they *never* come home."

He stands up and comes across to me. He grips my elbow and looks at me hard. "Believe me, son," Mr Conyers says, "you don't want to stab anyone. You do, and it'll haunt you till the day you die. I *know*."

Chapter 9

A Result

He's right, old Conyers. I think about it in bed on Tuesday night. Cecil's got a mum. A plain, ordinary mum in cheap clothes. He hasn't got a dad, so Cecil's all she's got. He's a nasty piece of work, but I bet his mum loves him to bits.

I think about the knife as well. Conyers' knife. It was here, in this room. I played with it, like a kid with a toy sword. But it's *not* a toy. It went in a guy's heart and stopped it. It took him away from his parents and messed up Conyers' life too. You can't feel good, touching a thing like that. You feel dirty.

Maybe that's why he hides it in a drawer, under all that rusty tat.

He doesn't tell on me, old Conyers. Even though I nicked his knife. I still do his garden, Tuesdays and Thursdays. By the time I've got it sorted, the slagging will have stopped. It's a bit better already. Cecil's mum has still got her boy, and my mum still has me.

If that's not a result, I don't know what is.

ROBERT SWINDELLS has written lots of page-turning, powerful novels that will grip you from the start ...

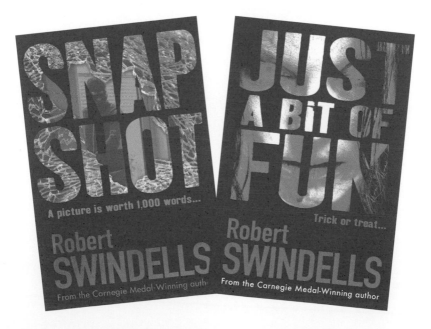

Our books are tested
for children and young people by
children and young people.

Thanks to everyone who consulted on
a manuscript for their time and effort in
helping us to make our books better
for our readers.